This Orchard book belongs to

____

____

____

700038602222

KT-572-108

For Little Jasmine, who loves gardening!

ORCHARD BOOKS
338 Euston Road, London NW1 3BH
Orchard Books Australia
Level 17/207 Kent Street, Sydney, NSW 2000

First published in 2011 by Orchard Books
First published in paperback in 2012

ISBN 978 1 40830 894 3

Text and illustrations © Caroline Jayne Church 2011

The right of Caroline Jayne Church to be identified as the author and illustrator of this work has been asserted by her in accordance with the Copyright, Designs and Patents Act, 1988.

A CIP catalogue record for this book is available from the British Library.

1 3 5 7 9 10 8 6 4 2

Printed in China

Orchard Books is a division of
Hachette Children's Books,
an Hachette UK company.
www.hachette.co.uk

Caroline Jayne Church

Nutmeg was in the garden making a daisy chain.

"Are you hungry, Nutmeg?" called Mum.

"What would you like to eat?"

"Shall we pick some apples from the tree?"

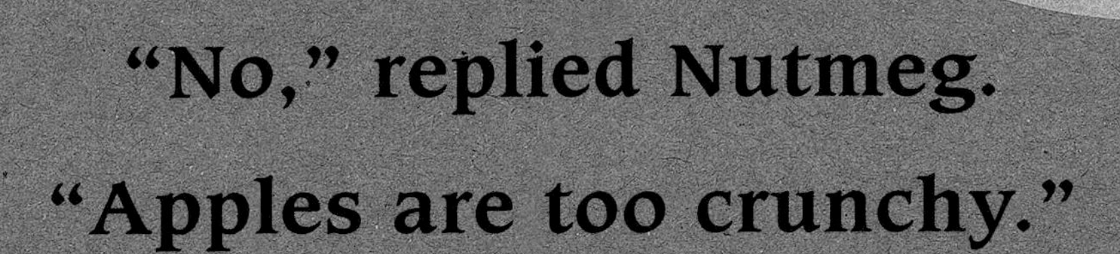

"No," replied Nutmeg.
"Apples are too crunchy."

"Then how about some pears?"
said Mum.

"Pears are a funny colour."
Nutmeg shook her head.

“Then how about peaches?”
asked Mum,
in a very patient voice.

“Peaches are too rough,”
answered Nutmeg.

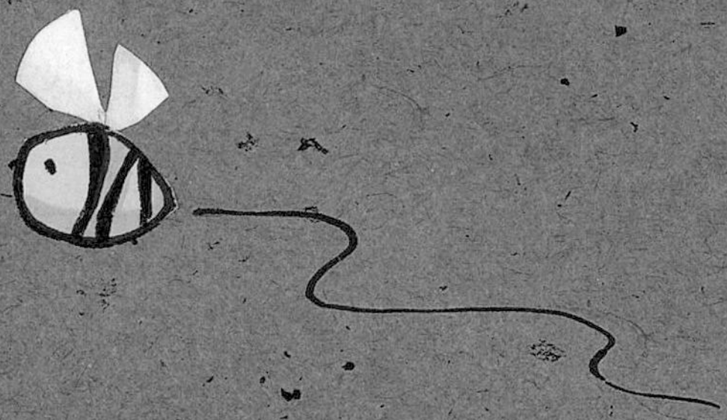

“What about bananas?” asked Mum.

“No, thank you,” replied Nutmeg.
“Bananas are far too squidgy!”

Mum looked
a little puzzled.

"You don't want apples . . .
they are too crunchy.

You don't want pears . . .
they are a funny
colour.

You don't want
peaches . . .
they are too rough!

And you don't want bananas . . .
they are too squidgy.

So, what DO you want to eat, Nutmeg?" asked Mum.

Nutmeg thought for
a moment . . .

“STRAWBERRIES!”

“I’ll make a special Strawberry Surprise,
just for you, Nutmeg,” said Mum.

Mum started chopping and peeling, slicing and dicing, as she prepared the very special Strawberry Surprise.

Nutmeg skipped off to finish her daisy chain.

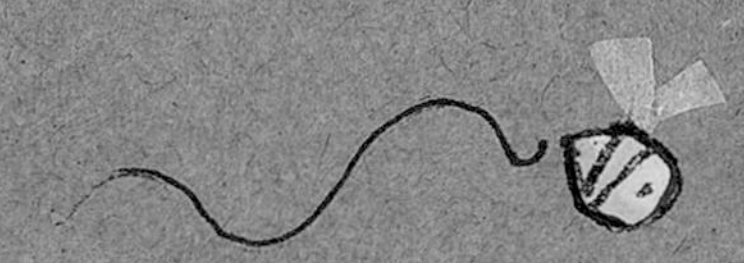

"Wow!"

YUM
YUM
YUM
YUM

YUM!

Nutmeg ate it all up!

"I'm going to call this

NUTMEG'S RAINBOW TREAT!"

**She gave Mum a big hug and said,
"Thank you for my Rainbow Treat . . .
please can we make it again tomorrow?"**